THIS BOOK BELONGS TO:

MW00942451

- - - - - - - - -

WHEN WE TOOK CAR TRIPS OR TRAIN
RIDES SEBASTIAN & I WOULD DRAW
PICTURES & THEN MAKE UP STORIES
ABOUT THEM. THE SILLIER THE BETTER!
HE INSPIRES ME STILL TODAY & I
DEDICATE THIS LITTLE BOOK TO HIM.

In Loving
Memory of
Sebastian
Pakis

you can shout

HELLO

and say

BUT hever

kiss a cactus!

YOU CAN KISS
YOUR FRIENDS

HELLO,

BYE BYE

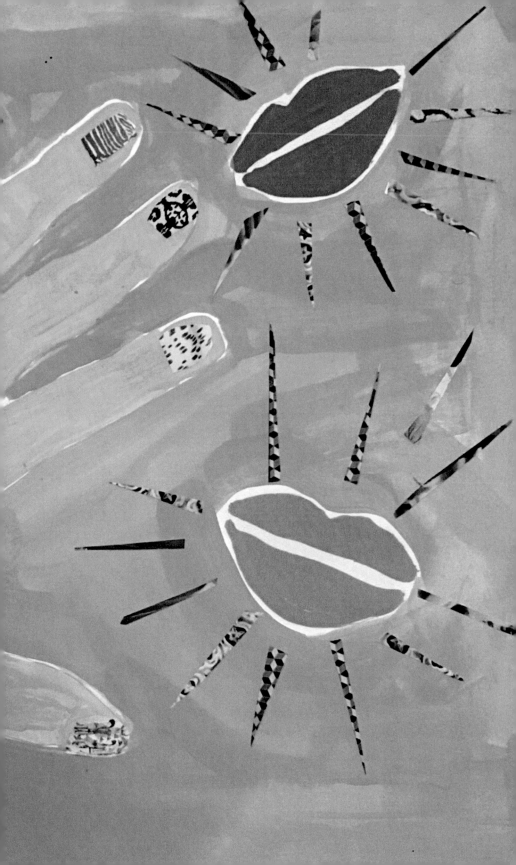

you can
kiss your
favorite
pizza pie

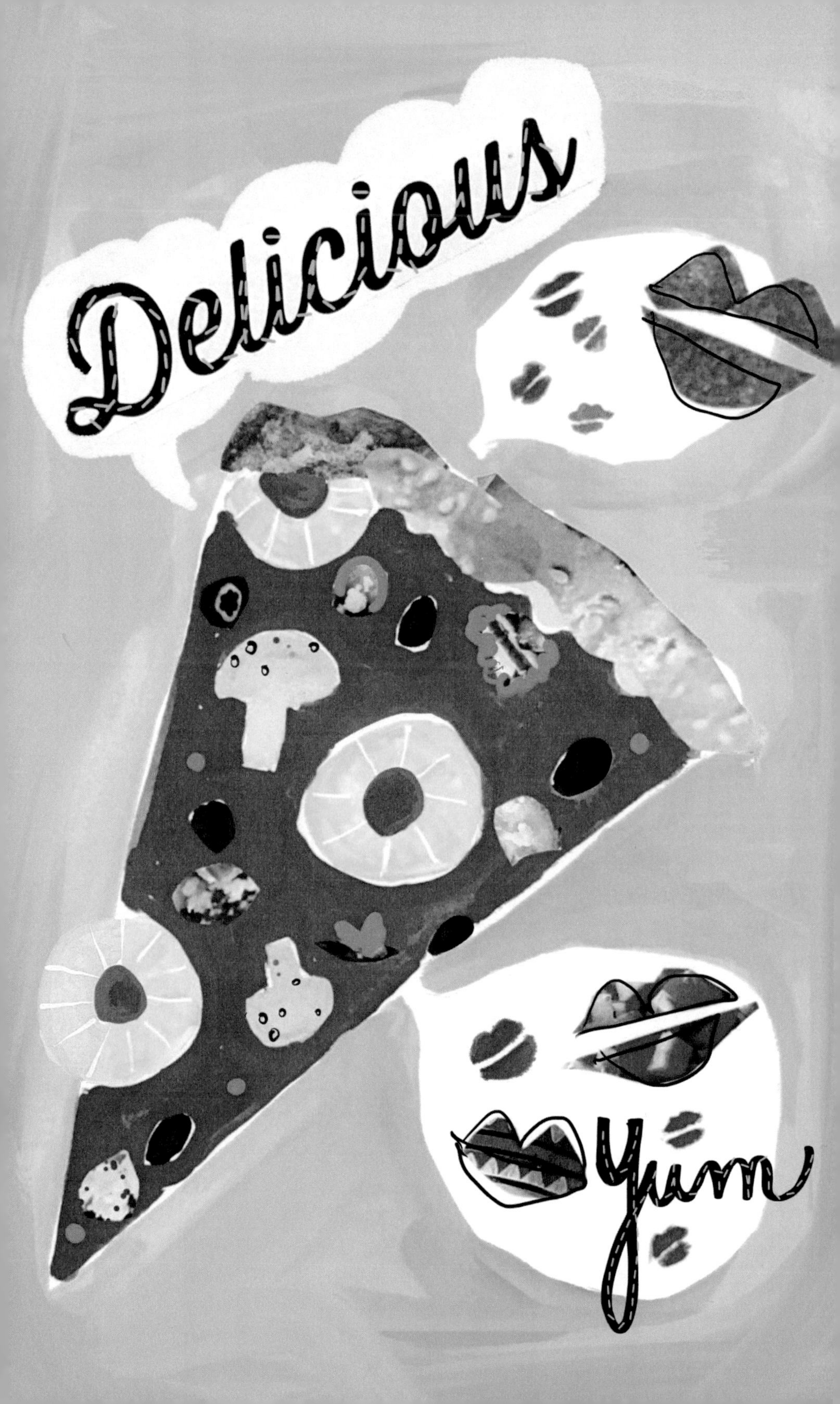
Delicious
Yum

YOU CAN KISS YOUR TOYS & TEDDY BEAR...

IF SHE SAYS SHE
DOESN'T CARE!

YOU CAN KISS A BOO BOO

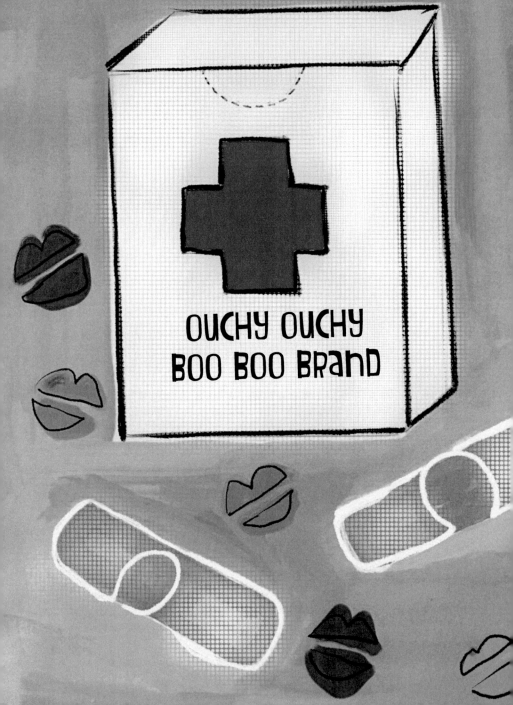

OUCHY OUCHY
BOO BOO BRAND

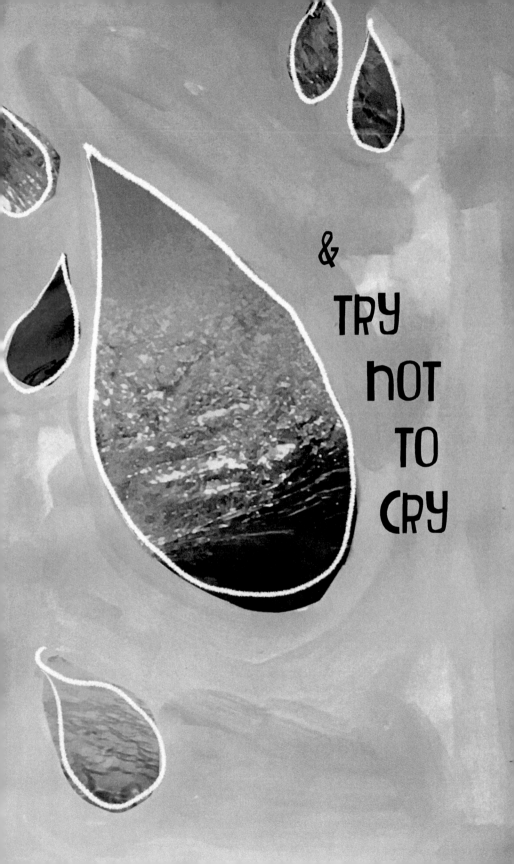

& TRY NOT TO CRY

you can be very

BRAVE

and give a big

BUT never

KiSS a CaCTUS

HOP INTO BED
& TURN OUT
THE LIGHT

BEFORE YOU
KNOW IT, THE SUN
WILL SHINE IN!

BLOW KISSES
TO THE
BIRDIES
AND ALL
THEIR KIN.

open your
arms &
KISS
THE SKY!
BUT FOR goodness
sake & me OH my...

never

kiss the
cacti!

NOW YOU DRAW A FUNNY CACTUS

DRAW A HAPPY CACTUS HERE

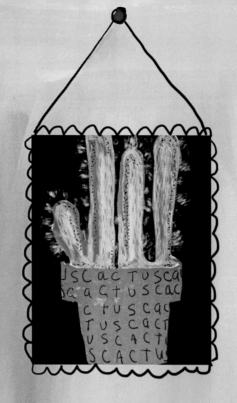

THANK YOU & XXX'S FROM MY HAPPY PLACE (AKA MY STUDIO) WHERE ALL MY PAINTS & PAPERS COME INTO BEING. EXXXTRA SPECIAL THANKS TO SAM SWINDELL FOR HIS PATIENCE & MAGICAL TECHNICAL SKILLS. WITHOUT HIM MY PILE OF PAINTINGS WOULD NEVER HAVE TURNED INTO THIS PRINTED FORM!

Love, jane